W9-BMH-627

GOING TO THE
FIREHOUSE

BY MERCER MAYER

Sandy Creek

An Imprint of Sterling Publishing
387 Park Avenue South
New York, NY 10016

ISBN 978-1-4351-2653-4

Manufactured in Dong Guan City, China
Lot #:
14 15 16 17 SCP 10 9 8 7
01/14

Today my class is going
to the firehouse!
I dress like a fireman.
Time to fight a fire!

This is Fireman Joe.

This is his dog, Sparky.

Sparky is a fire dog.

Fireman Joe has boots.

He has a jacket.

He has a helmet.

I have boots.

I have a jacket.

I do not have a helmet.

Joe slides down the pole.

Sparky howls.

That is what he does

when there is a fire.

We see a fire truck.

It is big.

It is red.

It has hoses and a ladder.

Joe checks the hoses.

He lets me help.

Whoosh goes the water.
This hose is working fine.

Joe checks the ladder.

He goes up and up.

He is in the sky.

Hello, Fireman Joe!

Joe checks the siren.

It goes Ooo! Eee! Ooo!

The siren is very loud.

I cover my ears.

Joe tells us about fires.

He tells us smoke goes up.

When smoke goes up,

we must go down to the floor.

I get on the floor.

Joe tells us what to do if we
are on fire.

Stop,

drop,

and roll!

I stop, drop, and roll!

Fireman Joe smiles.

He has a surprise.

26

He reaches into his truck.

Helmets for everyone!

I put on my helmet.

Joe tells me I will be
a good fireman one day.

Ding! Ding! goes the fire alarm.

I wave good-bye to Fireman Joe.

I wave good-bye to Sparky.

Time to fight a fire!

Fireman Joe is ready to go!

Sparky is, too.